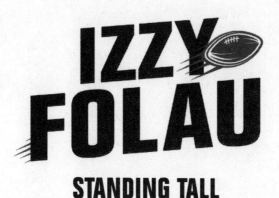

STANDING TALL

IZZY FOLAU

STANDING TALL

WRITTEN BY
DAVID HARDING

ILLUSTRATED BY
JAMES FOSDIKE

RANDOM HOUSE AUSTRALIA

A Random House book
Published by Random House Australia Pty Ltd
Level 3, 100 Pacific Highway, North Sydney NSW 2060
www.randomhouse.com.au

Penguin
Random House
Australia

First published by Random House Australia in 2015

Random House Books is part of the Penguin Random House group of companies
whose addresses can be found at global.penguinrandomhouse.com.

National Library of Australia
Cataloguing-in-Publication Entry

Creator: Harding, David, author
Title: Standing tall/David Harding and Israel Folau; illustrated by James Fosdike
ISBN: 978 0 85798 667 2 (pbk)
Series: Izzy Folau; 4
Target audience: For primary school age
Subjects: Rugby Union football – Tournaments – New South Wales – Juvenile fiction.
        Rugby Union football players – New South Wales – Juvenile fiction.
        Rugby football coaches – New South Wales – Juvenile fiction.
        Rugby Union football – New South Wales – Juvenile fiction.
Other creators/contributors: Folau, Israel, author; Fosdike, James, illustrator
Dewey number: A823.4

Illustrations by James Fosdike
Front cover image of Israel Folau by Chris Hyde/Getty Images
Back cover image of Israel Folau by Matt King/Getty Images
Cover design by Christabella Designs
Internal design and typesetting by Midland Typesetters, Australia
Printed in Australia by Griffin Press, an accredited ISO AS/NZS 14001:2004
Environmental Management System printer

Random House Australia uses papers that are natural, renewable and recyclable products
and made from wood grown in sustainable forests. The logging and manufacturing
processes are expected to conform to the environmental regulations of the country of
origin.

SIONE

'One, two, three . . . *Oof!* One, two, three . . .
Oof!'

Sione and his friends sat along the picket
fence surrounding the oval, watching on as
another rep team trained. They'd wandered
in to take a sneak peek at the stadium
and had come across the players dressed in

1

blue-and-white jerseys. Their moves and exercises were so regimented that their coach just stood in the middle of them, counting to three – the signal for the front row of boys to run and tackle giant pads – over and over.

The players grunted as they slammed into their imaginary opponents again and again. The boys were large and their voices deep.

Sione gulped. *They look like a pack of hungry lions*, he thought to himself.

'I'm not sure I want to face them on the field,' TJ murmured.

Sione nodded, unable to tear his eyes away.

'They seem to know what they're doing, that's for sure,' Eric agreed, leaning back on the fence.

'They're tough,' Adam said, impressed.

'They're big,' Steven said.

'They're show-offs,' Daniel snapped, jumping down from the fence.

Sione wasn't sure if he agreed with that. This rep team looked so . . . *professional*. But he was used to disagreeing with his friend's point of view. Daniel's bluntness and pride had been off-putting at first, but after their two-week cross-country tour, Sione had come to appreciate Daniel's insights and his passion for rugby.

The coach blew his whistle and, within moments, his players had formed a circle around him, kneeling on one leg and looking up at him with undivided attention.

'Listen up, boys!' the coach shouted. 'This is *your* time! This is *your* place! I've trained you right and made you ready, now it's up to you to pay me back with victories! You deserve to be state champions – and you will be – and I deserve to be a championship-winning coach. Our training has finished, tomorrow the battles begin.'

One of the players in blue spotted Sione watching them and winked. Sione wasn't sure what the wink meant, but he doubted it was a friendly hello. Sione turned away and walked after Daniel as the voice of the other team's coach echoed around the rugby complex.

Daniel and Sione made their way back to the patch of grass in front of the main stadium's entrance, where the rest of their team was waiting. Dwarfed by the grandstand, the team sat around excitedly discussing how cool it was going to be to play there. Next door was the ground Daniel and Sione had visited. During the State Championships both grounds would be in constant use.

Harrison looked up as the boys walked over. 'What was the other team like?' he asked.

'They thought they were great,' Daniel said.

Sione flopped down onto the grass and lay with his head resting on his training bag. He folded his hands under his head and gazed up at the blue sky. It was strange to be so close to home again. The last fortnight had been such an adventure. Two weeks ago Sione hadn't been on an aeroplane except for when he was a baby. Since then, he'd been on three.

Just last night I was up among those clouds, he thought. *I can't believe we're finally here at the State Championships!* Sione resisted the urge to pinch himself.

The Valley representative team had been on a tour to Queensland and the Northern Territory. They had played many games, worked on honing their skills and had become as close as family in the process.

It had been awesome – not just because they'd ridden on roller-coasters, been to beaches and seen real crocodiles, but because they'd done it all as a team, under the guidance of their fantastic mentor and coach, Wallaby Izzy Folau.

'Sorry about the wait, guys!' Izzy yelled, jogging over to the team. 'I've got the training schedule and some other info. We're ready to go.'

He handed Jeremy Fisk, the team manager, a folder of information and began giving out lanyards to everyone.

Sione pulled his lanyard over his head and examined the plastic card hanging from it. Their team name, Valley, was printed on one side in large letters, and on the other side was the Championships logo.

'Cool,' Daniel said, standing next to him.

Sione smiled. He couldn't wait to take a picture of it to show his family.

'You have to wear these at all times,' Izzy explained, 'except when playing and training, of course. Without it, you won't be allowed into change rooms and other areas closed off to the public.'

Sione picked up his gear, eager to start the day's training session.

'We're on Oval One,' Jeremy said, reading the paperwork. A few Valley players groaned. 'Don't worry,' he laughed, 'we'll get to play on the main ground, too.'

The team made their way to the oval, where the boys in the blue kit were now picking up their equipment.

'How's everyone going?' Izzy asked his team. 'Not too tired after our late night, I hope.'

'Russell! Russell!' Everyone's faces turned in the direction of the gruff voice. 'Watch what you're doing, Russell! Wake up!'

The other team's coach was yelling at one of his players, who had dropped a stack of coloured cones on the grass.

Valley stood outside the gate and waited for the other team to come off the ground. As they did, the players in blue stared at them and Izzy. For the first time, no one came up to ask Izzy for his autograph or just to say hello. Instead, the boys puffed out their chests and walked past as if Valley didn't exist. One or two of them even laughed.

Sione wondered what their problem was.

'Who do they think they are?' Daniel whispered in Sione's ear. 'We're just as good as them.'

'Who says?' A huge boy wearing a blue-and-white jersey towered over Daniel and Sione, a football under one arm.

Sione was taken aback.

'You don't look that good to me,' the boy continued, 'and your coach is overrated.'

'What?' Daniel shouted angrily. He lunged at the boy.

Sione grabbed Daniel's shoulders, holding him back. 'Don't,' he said. 'It's not worth it.'

'Mick! Let it go!' the boy's coach yelled.

Izzy ran over and positioned himself between the two boys. 'Steady on, guys. What's going on here?'

The boy in the blue jersey smirked. 'Your player just attacked me for no reason.'

'He's a liar!' Daniel yelled, his face burning.

'I'm sure this is all a misunderstanding,' Izzy said calmly. 'Let's shake hands and start over.'

'Mick, get out of here,' the other coach barked, as he walked past them. He glanced at Izzy. 'I trust this isn't an indication that your boys will be trouble at this tournament.'

Izzy shook his head. 'No, of course not. I'm Iz–'

'I know who you are,' the coach said and, ignoring Izzy's outstretched hand, stalked off.

Izzy shrugged and led the way to the centre of the oval. Daniel, still breathing heavily, had calmed down enough to walk without Sione holding onto him. He said nothing.

Tom and Mary Parker, the team's chaperones, came alongside Daniel and Sione. 'Try to not let it get to you,' Tom said gently. 'They just want to intimidate you and put you off your game.'

Daniel nodded.

When they reached the middle, everyone gathered around to listen to Izzy.

'We'll only be training here for an hour before the meeting with all the rep teams in the grandstand over there.' Izzy pointed to the imposing structure on the neighbouring ground. 'So let's make the most of the next sixty minutes.'

Sione smiled. *We've made it*, he thought. *We've actually made it!*

'Valley, welcome to the State Championships!' Izzy announced with a grin.

The boys cheered and pumped their fists before running off in all directions, their arms spread wide like the wings of a plane.

Tom and Mary Parker laughed.

With the sun in his eyes and the grass beneath his feet, Sione joined in with the others, running with glee across the pitch.

DANIEL

Showered and warm after a hard training session, the Valley boys stood with about two hundred other people outside the main entrance to the stadium. There was chatter and excitement among the eight teams as boys compared lanyards and swapped stories.

Daniel was more excited than most. He slung his bag over his shoulder and grinned with anticipation, reliving the moment after their training session when he'd been asked to bring his match kit to the tournament briefing.

'As everyone has probably realised,' Izzy had said, 'we don't have a team captain. We haven't really needed one, playing trial games, but it's a requirement of the State Championships. Each team needs a captain for the toss, to communicate with the referees on the field and to guide the team off it. Besides, you need a captain to hold up the winner's trophy in all the photos after the Grand Final!'

The boys had cheered at this.

'After a lot of thought,' Izzy continued, 'I'm sure you'll all agree that Daniel Masters should be captain.'

The entire team broke into applause and whistles.

'I knew it!' Sione had exclaimed, clapping him on the back.

It had been awesome and, for some reason, much sweeter than being named captain for his school team.

At the start of the tour, Daniel had expected that he would be named captain – that he deserved it and no one else did – because of his skill and prowess on the field. Since then, with the help of Izzy and his teammates, he had learned the true nature of leadership and the need to be a respectful role model, not just a great player.

Sione elbowed Daniel, jerking him back to reality. 'Those guys are still staring at us,' he said out of the corner of his mouth.

Daniel shrugged. 'Let them.'

The crowd around them surged as boys tried to get closer to Izzy. Izzy showed no favourites, saying hello and high-fiving all of them. While each team was supposedly in opposition to one another, this wasn't the case in Izzy's eyes. Daniel knew from firsthand experience that Izzy wanted his players to have fun above all else. Kids were smiling, happy to be standing near the famous Wallaby.

The big glass doors opened and everyone was ushered inside. Around a corner and

18

through another set of doors was a room that looked like a movie theatre. A large screen hung above a stage at the front of the room, and facing them was row upon row of cushioned seats.

'Wow, are we going to see a movie?' Adam asked no one in particular. 'This just keeps getting better!'

A group of men and women dressed in suits stood on the stage and watched the boys file in. Once everyone was seated, one of the men stepped forward. He was wearing dark-rimmed glasses and a grey suit. He held up his hand and the crowd immediately hushed. 'Welcome to the annual State Junior Rugby Championships!' he announced.

Many people clapped and whistled at this. Daniel smiled and sank into his comfy chair.

'Before we get into the details of the competition,' the man continued, 'we have a short video to show you. Enjoy.' He walked off the stage and sat in the front row. The lights promptly turned off and the big screen flickered to life.

'Anybody got popcorn?' Jake whispered down the row.

'Even if I did I wouldn't trust you with it,' Daniel laughed, remembering the mess Jake made of his dinner one night.

Daniel returned his attention to the screen. First came the inspiring soundtrack, then the scenes from previous Championships and footage of boys playing for their clubs.

Line-out jumps, goal kicks, sprints down the flank – it was all there. The boys in the videos grew older and older until, towards the end, Daniel realised they were watching clips of the Australian rugby team playing in front of huge crowds. Izzy even featured in the clip, scoring a try and waving to the crowd. The entire Valley team cheered for their mentor. Then the video faded away to reveal the State Championships logo and the words 'Tomorrow's heroes, today'.

When the lights came on again, the audience applauded. The air was electric with the boys' excitement. Daniel could have watched it a hundred times without getting bored.

The man in the grey suit stood up again and approached the microphone. 'I'm glad you enjoyed the video,' he said. His eyes swept the crowd, causing every boy to take a deep breath in anticipation. 'You have all worked hard to get here. Congratulations on making it this far.'

The man went on to explain the rules and housekeeping matters. Daniel saw Jeremy in the row in front of him taking notes. Then the competition draw appeared on the screen. Daniel, along with every other boy in the room, immediately scanned it for his team.

'You'll see from this diagram,' continued the speaker, 'that there are eight rep teams from across the state. Each one has been randomly placed in one of two groups of four. Over the next couple of days you will play all the other teams in your group once, which brings you to a total of three games. The two semi-finals will be held on Saturday and will be played by the top two teams of each group. On Sunday we'll have the Grand Final and name our champion team. Don't worry if you get knocked out after your three pool games – everyone has tickets to the Grand Final.'

One of the other officials then stood up to talk. She mentioned that the players' family members would be given tickets to every match and access to the teams between games. Daniel wondered what his dad would look like sitting high up in the stands. He imagined his mum sitting next to his dad and watching Daniel raise the winner's trophy, but he didn't have the guts to dream that big.

Daniel turned to look at Sione, sure that he was thinking the same thing. They both lived away from their mums and Daniel knew that it was just as painful for Sione as it was for him.

After the briefing, everyone except the team captains left the theatre and returned to their hotel rooms. Mary came over to sit with Daniel to keep him company during the photo shoot.

'Are you excited?' she asked with a smile.

Daniel nodded. If he was honest, he felt kind of nervous. 'Definitely.'

The eight team captains were asked to change into their kits and then ushered onto the stage in front of the movie screen. A photographer then assembled them in various arrangements and took what seemed like a thousand photos. Daniel grinned throughout the photo shoot, proud of his Valley green. He wondered what newspapers and websites the captains' photo might appear in.

The entire time, however, Daniel had to avoid Mick's eyes. He stood as far away from him as the photographer would allow, and when Mick said something to Daniel about beating him on the field, he pretended not to hear him. Daniel kept his eyes on Mary, who was watching the shoot from the front row of seats.

Afterwards, he felt a tap on his right shoulder. Daniel turned around and found himself face to face with Mick.

'You think that just because you have Izzy Folau you're better than us?' Mick hissed.

Daniel groaned inwardly. *What was this guy's problem?*

'Well, don't,' Mick sneered. 'We're better than you will ever be. Got that?' He pushed Daniel as he walked past him.

That was the final straw. Daniel clenched his fists and tore after him. He was furious.

'Daniel, stop!' Mary called.

Reluctantly, Daniel halted in his tracks as Mary ran up to him.

'Listen, he's just trying to get under your skin. But you're better than that, right?' she said. 'You're the Valley team captain and you're at the State Championships. How cool is that? Don't ruin it by getting into trouble.'

'But he's being so mean!' Daniel said through gritted teeth.

'He may be,' Mary conceded, 'but why don't we let our football do the talking, rather than our fists?'

Daniel looked down at his hands and unfurled his fingers. He sighed. 'Tries and goals may break our souls but names will never hurt me.'

Mary nodded and put an arm around him. 'That's the spirit.'

Laughing, the two of them headed out of the stadium together.

SIONE

Daniel, Jake, Adam and Sione were huddled around Adam's iPad, watching the latest rugby match live from Europe. Their heads were practically touching in order to get a good view of the footage on the tiny screen.

'France won't win now,' Jake said. 'There's a minute to go and they're six points behind.'

Adam groaned. 'Yeah, might as well turn it off.'

'No, wait,' Daniel said. 'Look, there's an opening.'

The ball leaves the back of the scrum . . . Lacroix passes it to Dutrait . . . tackled but somehow passes it out the back to Varnes, who's through! Like an arrow from a bow, something from nothing, Varnes steams towards the tryline. Benito is chasing — and Romeo — but there's no hope for them. Varnes is home, scores under the post. An amazing effort!

The four boys cheered, their favourite team for the match was now only one point behind with seconds to play.

. . . And a beautiful kick for goal by Gaspard. Never in doubt. The crowd is going crazy. What a win for their national team!

Sione fell back onto the bed. He wondered if one day someone would be watching him play for his country. Adam switched off his iPad and yawned.

'None of that,' Jake ordered. 'We're not going to bed yet. This is our third-last night together, so let's hang out some more.'

'Yeah, let's,' Daniel said.

Sione was conflicted. He wanted to keep hanging out with the boys but he also knew how important it was to get a good night's sleep before a big game.

'I don't know,' Adam said, voicing Sione's concern. 'We have two games tomorrow. I think we should get as much sleep as we can.'

'But that's so boring,' Jake moaned.

'I have that rugby card game,' Adam offered. 'I'm brushing my teeth now, but we could play that quickly before bed.'

'Fine,' Jake relented.

Sione and Daniel began rummaging through their bags for their pyjamas.

'Hey, Sione,' Adam chuckled, his mouth full of toothpaste suds, 'remember how you used to carry Izzy's email around in your bag?'

'What do you mean "used to"?' Jake laughed. 'That was only a week ago!'

Sione laughed and rolled his eyes. 'Three nights left . . .' he whispered to himself. He remembered how he'd fought back tears while boarding the bus to go on tour. He never expected he would have to do it again when it was time to return home.

In the last two weeks, Sione had noticed a change in himself and he knew the others did too. Though he was still quiet, he was much more assured now. He found it easier to make friends and he was less worried about what others thought of him. Sione had shared a lot about his personal life with Daniel, too, and that was something he had never trusted anyone with before.

He wasn't the only one who'd changed. Daniel had also learned a lot about himself over the past couple of weeks. Sione could barely stand him when they'd first met, but now he was certain they'd be friends forever. Sione knew he would never forget this trip.

He slid his hand into the side of his bag and felt around for the printout of Izzy's email.

There was still a bit of blu-tack on it. He taped it on the wall near his pillow and went back to searching for his pyjamas.

'Hey, he still has it!' Jake said, pointing at the email.

The other boys laughed and Sione grinned proudly.

Once all four boys were ready for bed, they sat on the floor and Adam pulled out his rugby card game. He shuffled the deck and dealt a hand of cards to everyone.

'I'll start,' Daniel announced.

Jake smacked his forehead. 'Why do you always get to go first?'

Daniel shrugged. 'I called it.'

'Fine, whatever,' Jake laughed, shaking his head.

'Tries,' Daniel said.

Sione looked at his cards. They each had a famous rugby player from the past or the present. Below their pictures were lists of their playing stats. The player he held who had scored the most tries was Rory Underwood with fifty.

'Fifty,' he said.

'Forty-six,' said Jake.

'Forty,' said Adam.

Daniel held up his hand, displaying his card triumphantly. 'Sorry, guys, David Campese with sixty-four tries.'

The others groaned and handed over their cards. They played a few more rounds, comparing famous players and arguing over whose was the best when there was a light knock at the door. Sione got up to open it.

'Hi, guys,' Izzy said, walking in. 'Sorry for interrupting your game, but we have two massive matches tomorrow. Lights out in five minutes.'

'Did you know that Jonny Wilkinson scored one thousand, two hundred and forty-six points in his career?' Daniel asked him, holding up the card to prove it.

'Yes, I did,' Izzy said, grinning, 'but that's still not as many as Dan Carter. Or as many as Daniel Masters will kick by the end of his career.'

Daniel blushed.

'Lights out in five, okay?' Izzy said. 'See you tomorrow, bright and early.'

He left, and the four friends were soon in their beds.

'Jake, who's coming from your family to watch us?' Adam said into the darkness.

'I don't know. Pretty much everyone, I guess. What about you?'

Adam counted off each of his immediate family members. 'Mum, Dad, James, Chris and my grandparents.'

'Cool,' Jake said. 'Who's coming from your family, Daniel?'

But Daniel didn't answer. As the question hung in the air, Sione wondered if he really was asleep or just pretending.

DANIEL

The change room was a hive of activity as the team prepared for their first match of the Junior Rugby State Championships. When all the boys were dressed in their kit, Izzy clapped to get everyone's attention. 'We have ten minutes. Everyone sit down, please.'

The boys scurried to sit on a bench or on the floor in front of Izzy, some of them still lacing up their boots.

Sione sat next to Daniel. 'I can't believe this place, it's like we're professionals already,' he whispered. 'It's a *real* change room!'

Daniel nodded, watching Izzy as he prepared to speak.

Jake, who was sitting on the other side of Daniel, added, 'And this isn't even the main stadium. Imagine what it's like in there!'

'Settle down, boys,' Izzy called above the excited chatter. 'We have to get out there for the warm-up and pre-match festivities, but I just wanted to say a few things before we do.'

A calm immediately settled upon the room as the talk ceased and all eyes turned to Izzy.

'This weekend is the culmination of a lot of hard work,' Izzy continued. 'I want to thank you for all your efforts on this tour. You should be very proud of yourselves. We have been through so much together and we now know each other so well. In a way, we are now family. We've played games in three different states and territories, we've ridden roller-coasters and we've watched crocodiles eat their lunch.'

Some of the boys chuckled at this.

'But,' Izzy said, pausing for effect, 'what happens here over the next two or three days will probably be the main memories you

41

will carry with you for the rest of your life. You might forget the colour of the walls in your cabin on the Gold Coast, but you will probably not forget how you played at the State Championships.'

Daniel swallowed.

'Win, lose or draw,' Izzy said, 'I want you to play your hardest, try your best and have no regrets. Keep your eyes on the prize but remember to enjoy the game. Above all, we are here for the love of the game.'

The boys clapped and cheered in response. Daniel was surprised to find himself so emotional over this.

'We would like to say something, too,' Tom Parker piped up. He put an arm around Mary, who was standing next to him. 'We're so proud of you. No matter the result, you're all fantastic.'

'Oh, and we have a surprise for you up in the grandstand,' Mary added, a glint in her eye. 'Go, Crocs!'

The boys laughed. It seemed the nickname Tom and Mary had given the team during their time in the Northern Territory had stuck. Daniel couldn't imagine what the surprise might be.

Izzy stepped back and gave the floor to Jeremy. Daniel wondered what he was going to say. Jeremy didn't usually speak to them before a game. He carried pens and paper and told them what hotel room to sleep in and what plane to catch. What could he possibly say to motivate them?

'Uh . . . hi, everyone,' Jeremy began. 'What Tom and Mary and Izzy said is all true.'

Is that it? Daniel thought impatiently, eager to get out on the field.

'I just wanted to say that I've been in your position. I've played in State Championships. Almost every year I made a rep team some-where. I even played for my state and for Australia at the junior level – in rugby league and rugby union.'

Daniel's jaw dropped. He'd had no idea Jeremy was that good. He turned to look at Sione to gauge his reaction but Sione just nodded at him. *How did he know this already?* Daniel thought.

'I played in many great teams,' Jeremy continued, 'but I never won a premiership.

I never got a medal. My teams never won a championship or competition of any kind.' The room was completely silent. 'It's okay, I still played hard and was happy, but I can't deny I wish I had won something just once. So, even though I hope you all get to see many championships, play hard today. Don't take your opportunities for granted. Let's do this!'

Everyone cheered and clapped and Daniel knew they were ready to take to the field. As the boys strode out of the change room, they chanted their name loud and proud.

'Val-ley! Val-ley! Val-ley!'

The loudspeaker screeched to life. 'Welcome to today's game – Valley against Metro,' the announcer bellowed. 'Please rise for the national anthem.'

Goosebumps crept up along Daniel's arms as the first notes of 'Advance Australia Fair' blared all around him. His team was standing in a straight line, facing the small crowd in the grandstand. Somewhere to the left of him, Metro were doing the same. With his hands by his sides, Daniel sang the anthem through. Afterwards, the main referee motioned for Daniel to stand next to him. The Metro captain, dressed in their trademark yellow jersey, was called upon to do the same. The referee stood between them and produced a twenty-cent coin for the toss.

Daniel could hardly believe this was happening. He called tails and won the toss. Sticking to the game plan, he selected to receive the ball in the first half. Jogging back to his teammates to tell them that first piece of good news felt amazing.

While Daniel stood in position, awaiting the starting whistle, a low murmur rumbled through the crowd. Daniel looked up and scanned the stands to work out what was going on – and then he spotted them. Tom and Mary Parker were in the middle of a group of Valley family members dressed in head-to-toe green, some shaking green pompoms and all cheering for 'the Crocs'. Mary was even waving a green sign with a crocodile on it and the words 'Go, Crocs!' Thanks to Tom and Mary, Daniel felt like the game was as exciting as an international test. He grinned and waved at them.

But where's Mum and Dad? he wondered.

Eventually, Daniel spied his father. He was sitting far away from the parents in green and watching his son intently. Daniel wished he would join in with the other parents but he knew that wasn't his dad's thing at all. His dad preferred to study the game without distraction and make a mental note of all the ways Daniel could improve for next time. He told himself his mum was probably sitting somewhere else or running late, but in his heart he knew better.

After the excitement of the pre-game festivities, the match started with a bang.

The second Daniel received the ball, he was taken down in a thumping tackle by an opposition forward, leaving him wheezing on the ground. But after that Daniel fell into a comfortable and familiar rhythm as he played. The team performed as Izzy had taught them. They played hard and to the plan. Set plays were completed, tries were scored. Daniel saw his dad clapping after one of his goal kicks and that was probably the highlight of the day for him. It was a smooth game.

But there was one moment Daniel would never forget. He threw an awesome cut-out pass to Sione on the wing. The ball skipped the hands of three other Valley backs, totally confusing the defending team. Sione found himself in the clear with only Eric, their centre, in support. Sione could have scored a try in the corner but decided to pass the ball along to Eric at the last moment. Eric then went on to score under the posts as Metro defenders ran around him.

When it was all over, the Valley players were ecstatic. Some boys laughed with relief, some were stunned and some even cried tears of joy. They had won by a large margin: 31–8.

Daniel, however, remained calm. He told himself this was only the first game and that the matches would only get harder from here. Although his body was sore, he took the time as team captain to shake hands with the Metro players and to thank the referee. Daniel was sure his dad would be proud of the way he stayed in control, even after the game.

Walking off, Daniel glimpsed the score-board again and smiled. Perhaps he had been right all along. Valley were legit and were going to be hard to beat. He could almost feel the cold handles of the Championship trophy in his hands.

SIONE

'Boys, settle down,' Izzy called. 'We all need to stretch and stay warm. We have another game this afternoon.'

Sione sat in the corner feeling sorry for Izzy. It was the first time the team hadn't listened to him. Izzy had been trying to get their attention over and over again, but everyone was just too excited. They were all talking over the top of one another and re-enacting their favourite moments from the match. Sione figured that settling a group of twenty boys after a big win was next to impossible.

'Hey! Quiet! Izzy's speaking!' Daniel shouted. He was standing on one of the chairs scattered around the change room.

The room immediately fell silent and even Izzy seemed taken aback. A small smile tugged at the corners of Sione's mouth.

'Thank you, Daniel,' Izzy said. 'All right, everyone, you are allowed to be excited, but we have another game in a few hours and we need to make sure our bodies are ready for it. We will keep using the interchange bench regularly, but we want to do all we can to avoid any injury. Everyone, take a spot on the floor and do your stretches.'

The boys sighed and lowered themselves to the ground. Methodically, they began to stretch their hamstrings. The change room settled into an eerie quiet after the insanity of moments before.

Izzy chuckled. 'Guys, you're not in trouble,' he said. 'You can still talk.'

Without hesitation, the boys burst into another round of rehashings of the game. As Sione stretched, his mind could only dwell on one topic. He hadn't stopped scanning the stands for his family during the entire match, only half-focused on actually playing. At every opportunity Sione had looked for the familiar faces of his dad, aunty and sister without success. What made it worse was that every other Valley boy seemed to have at least one relative there to watch them play.

'Did you see your family?' he heard Eric ask Steven.

Steven looked at him like he was crazy. 'Of course! As if they wouldn't come.'

'My sister was there, and she's only a few months old,' Sean added.

All the boys talking about their families blended into one voice. 'They were decked out in green . . . It was so cool . . . Can't wait to see them again . . .'

The fact that Sione couldn't join in the conversation made him feel even more despondent.

'What's wrong?' Daniel asked, sitting down beside Sione to continue his stretches.

'Nothing,' Sione answered.

Daniel shook his head, unconvinced. 'We just won our first game and you're here in the corner hardly enjoying the win. Something's wrong – what is it?'

'Who cares about winning if the people you care about aren't there to see it?' Sione mumbled.

Daniel nodded as if he'd already guessed that was the case. 'If it makes you feel any better, my dad was there but he wasn't cheering with the others. He was probably on his phone half the time.'

'At least he was there,' Sione said. Tears welled in his eyes.

'Yeah, well, my mum wasn't.'

The two boys sat there in silence, angry at the world and now, for some reason, with each other.

Why can't I just be happy we won? Sione asked himself.

The change-room door rattled as someone knocked on it forcefully. Sione watched Jeremy open the double doors a fraction and have a word with someone standing in the hall. He turned back to the boys, looking for someone in particular. Jeremy's eyes met Sione's. 'Come over here, mate,' he said, motioning for Sione to get up.

Sione almost ran to him, hardly daring to guess who might be waiting outside. The door opened, and the euphoria he felt at that moment was unimaginable.

'Dad!' he shouted, jumping into his father's arms.

'Hi, son.' His dad laughed. 'You happy to see us or what?'

His aunty patted his back and hugged him too. Sione picked up Mele and spun her around, and it was then that he noticed the three of them were dressed in green. He smiled even wider, if that was at all possible,

and began telling them about everything that had happened on tour. Not halfway through his summary, his aunty and dad began laughing so hard he couldn't continue. He looked up at them wondering what was so funny.

'I'm sorry,' his aunty said, wiping her eyes, 'but this is some change in you, Sione. You haven't spoken this much in years!'

'There'll be time to catch up properly later,' his dad added. 'But we are so glad you've had such a good time.'

Mele waved a piece of paper at Sione. He took it from her and turned it around to see the drawing. There were lots of green scribbles and what looked like a person standing in the middle of it all.

'It's you! It's you!' Mele sang, dancing around.

Sione smiled. 'I'll keep it forever,' he promised. Not having any pockets, Sione folded it up and tucked it into his sock.

'Sorry we were so late,' Aunty sighed. 'Your dad couldn't get out of work as early as we'd hoped.'

'That's okay,' Sione said. 'There are heaps of games to go. We've got another one this afternoon.'

Aunty grinned. 'And we'll be back every day, we won't miss another game.'

Sione grinned back as Mele gave him a pinky promise and his dad ruffled his hair. So far, this was the best day of the tour!

SIONE

The whistle blew and Daniel kicked the ball deep into North West's territory. A player wearing a red jersey with a white collar effortlessly picked the ball out of the sky and powered upfield.

Sione looked the player straight in the eye as they ran towards each other. They were intense eyes — eyes that would have scared Sione if he saw them anywhere but on the rugby pitch. Sione steadied himself and slightly lowered his body, preparing to dive at the legs of the oncoming steamroller.

As Sione's shoulder slammed into the North West player, his arms wrapped around the boy's legs. It felt like he had tackled a

stone statue. Sione fell away, instantly sore and dizzy. Looking back with glassy eyes, he saw that his opponent hadn't even stopped. Wobbly but still on the move, it took the extra weight of Jake coming in from the side to finally take the player down.

Sione rubbed his shoulder and stood up gingerly. He ran back onside, averting his eyes from the grandstand. So eager to have his family watch him in the crowd before, he was now embarrassed to see the looks on their faces.

As he returned to the back line, the North West players began moving the ball forward. They would be brought down in a tackle only to move the ball on again. They kept coming, making slow but constant progress up the field, using strength and discipline alone.

It wasn't long before Sione was exhausted. His legs were tight and heavy, his body ached and his lungs were overworked. During a break in play, Jeremy ran onto the field with water for the team. Sione gulped it down before spraying some over his face in an attempt to wake himself up.

'Stay with it,' Jeremy said. 'You're going good.'

Sione nodded, though he wasn't so sure. His desire to keep his mind and body in check and to continue to push himself was dissipating. His feet, usually light and quick on the grass, were dragging as he struggled to keep up. It was hard being a full-time defender.

Why can't I keep up? he wondered. He'd been doing all those extra early-morning fitness sessions with Izzy to make sure he was at his fittest. *Has it all been a waste of time?*

And then, after what seemed like forever, Adam tackled a North West centre so hard that the ball popped loose from his grasp and unexpectedly found its way into Daniel's hands. He flicked the ball to Eric, who was then tackled. Nevertheless, the Valley team cheered and clapped. The onslaught was finally over – at least for the time being.

Sione gritted his teeth. He didn't want his family to have come all this way to see him struggling. *There's no way the car trip home is going to be a sad one*, he said to himself.

He sprinted off his line, took a pass cleanly and ran at the defence with new-found energy. The tackle was hard and the ground was harder, but Sione rolled over and planted the ball behind him. It was taken away by Harrison, and Sione was soon left to brush himself off.

'Run, tackle, run, tackle,' Daniel muttered as the boys walked off at half-time. 'This is crazy!'

Sione looked down as he passed the scoreboard. He already knew they were behind twelve points to seven but he didn't want to see it lit up in big numbers. He looked at the crowd instead and waved to his family. Mele put down a bucket of hot chips to wave back. Sione smiled as they disappeared from view and he walked inside their change room. He hoped there would be even more to smile about in the second half.

Everyone collapsed into the room. Some boys flopped down onto a bench, others just sank to the floor. They were all exhausted — even the interchange players. Sione did his best to keep moving. He knew that letting his muscles tighten during the break would make running in the second half even harder. He guzzled his water as he jogged on the spot, waiting for Izzy's message.

How they had even scored those seven points, Sione didn't know. It had all happened in a blur, against the flow of play. Jake had ended up with the ball after an intense scrum and he fell over the line. Daniel kicked his conversion and that was it. Besides that, North West had been in control the entire match. They had scored two tries and kicked one conversion.

'I'm glad they're only five points in front,' Daniel said.

It was definitely a positive, but Sione still couldn't see how they were going to win. North West was just too aggressive. Meeting them at their game was exhausting, let alone trying to rise above them.

'It's not fair,' Jake said, 'we had to play two games in a row. I don't have the energy.'

'But so did they,' Daniel reasoned. 'If we want to win the trophy, we have to beat them. We knew it was going to be tough.'

Jake groaned.

Izzy entered the room last, clapping and saying how proud he was of Valley's performance.

'They're playing at high intensity,' Izzy conceded, 'but this is what rep footy is all about. We're just five points down – you should all be so proud. I've seen nothing but fantastic efforts across the ground. We can do this!'

We've been playing well? Sione was stunned.

'We just have to lift and keep lifting,' Izzy added. 'Don't give up now – we are so close.' This got everyone sitting up straight and listening. 'We will be interchanging you a lot this half to keep you all fresh. Listen to instructions. The cleaner you come on and off, the easier it will be for everyone. Don't take an interchange as an insult – especially the forwards. Expect a break!'

'Thank goodness!' Jake wheezed, and all the boys laughed.

Valley dug deep to find the energy to hold back the North West onslaught. Like a tense chess match, the ball was moved around the field with neither team gaining a true advantage. The crowd was silent and on the edge of their seats. With just a few minutes left in the second half, North West were looking rattled. Their offensive pushes had not resulted in more points. Though, as long as they stayed in front, it didn't really matter.

With two minutes left in the game, Valley seemed destined to lose. *At least we can go to bed tonight proud of our efforts*, Sione told himself.

Then the ball landed in his hands. With his body sore and his mind numb, Sione was unsure of what to do next. He fumbled it over the touchline to his left. The crowd and his teammates groaned in disappointment. Sione was devastated.

Valley won the line-out, and Daniel surprised everyone by passing the ball back to the blind side of play and into Sione's hands.

With seconds left in the match and nothing to lose, Sione started running through the remnants of the line-out, and then . . . he was on his own. Like a wave rolling back from the beach, there was suddenly nothing but a vast emptiness in front of him. The crowd roared and, moments later, Sione was over the tryline.

Daniel kicked the simplest of conversions and that was that. The Crocs had won by two points! Sione pumped his fist and faced the stand where his family was jumping up and down, cheering. He had never smiled so wide.

DANIEL

The change room was packed full of the players' families hugging and applauding every member of the Valley team. Everyone was ecstatic. Daniel's dad was the last to enter the room. He was dressed in his trademark suit and tie, just in case he was called into the office. 'That was excellent!' he said, ruffling Daniel's hair.

'Thanks,' Daniel replied, grinning from ear to ear.

'I am so proud of you. You put in one hundred and ten per cent today. There were some junior selectors watching, you know. I just had a chat with them outside about you,' his dad said, tapping the side of his nose.

Daniel bit his lip, imagining all kinds of embarrassing things his dad would have said. He took a deep breath, knowing exactly what was coming next.

'But,' his dad continued, 'there are some things I want you to work on for tomorrow.'

Daniel's shoulders slumped.

His dad pulled out his phone to look at the notes he'd taken during the game. 'Three things, really. First, get the team around you more. You're the captain, remember? Keep up communication, get them into huddles, let them know your expectations . . .'

Daniel's mind drifted back to the game. *How did we survive that one?* he wondered.

The two games that day had been so different. Daniel was immensely proud that his team had not only won both of them, but that they had overcome many obstacles to do so. What's more, Valley was now on top of their half of the ladder. Winning tomorrow would secure their place in the semis.

When his dad finally finished speaking, Daniel said what he always said: 'Okay, Dad. I'll try.'

He glanced over at Sione's family. They looked happy and there were so many of them compared to his family of two.

'Where's Mum?' he asked.

'What do you mean? You know where,' his dad replied, frowning.

'She's not here?'

'Not as far as I know. Why would she be?'

Because I wrote her an email asking her to come! Daniel shouted in his mind. *Because she wants to watch me play? Because she loves me?* 'I don't know,' he said, his eyes dropping to the ground.

'Hello again, Mr Masters,' Izzy said, walking up to them. He smiled and held out his hand to Daniel's dad.

Mr Masters shook his hand firmly. 'You've done well with this team. That was some performance out there.'

'Thank you,' Izzy replied, 'but the boys are the ones we should congratulate. They played out of their skin – especially Daniel, here.'

'Very true,' Mr Masters agreed. His phone began to ring, and he excused himself to answer it. 'I'll see you tomorrow,' he called over his shoulder.

Daniel nodded and waved goodbye. While all his teammates were still celebrating with their families, he found himself a quiet corner and sat down on a bench. He decided not to let it get him down. He knew his dad loved him in his own way.

Shortly after dinner Jake made a chance discovery at the hotel. Near the main foyer was a room entirely dedicated to table tennis. Once news spread, the whole team crammed into the room, playing a game or waiting their turn, cheering every hit as well as every miss.

Daniel swung at the ball, sending it back towards Adam and Jake with a delightful *ping*. He was playing alongside Sione, and with his hoodie up over his head he felt warm and relaxed after an exhausting day.

Jake hit the ball to Sione.

'So how'd you guys have so much energy out there today?' Daniel asked them.

'Shh!' Jake hissed as the ball flew past his bat. 'You're trying to distract us.'

'Ten to nine,' Sione announced.

'No, seriously,' Daniel said, 'where did all your energy come from?'

'I think I was afraid to stop,' Adam said with a shrug. 'I knew that if I stopped I might not start again.'

Everyone laughed.

'Yeah, I didn't want to let everyone down,' Jake admitted.

Gradually, the two forwards' focus seemed to evaporate, and Sione and Daniel were named the victors, with fifteen points to nine.

Sione went to sit on a bench as other boys took their places for the next match. Daniel sat next to him and yawned.

'All that talking about tiredness is making me sleepy,' Sione said. 'I'm ready to pack it in.'

Daniel tried to speak but yawned instead. He was forced to simply nod in agreement. 'But can you believe it?' he said. 'We won two games and have a chance of getting to the finals. *The finals!*'

Sione smiled. 'I know. Imagine if we hadn't won them. How different would tonight feel?'

'Even if we had lost, if I felt as tired as this I'd know I'd tried my best,' Daniel said. 'I'd be sad but I'd still be holding my head up.'

'You sound more like Izzy every day,' Sione laughed.

Daniel grinned.

'I kind of feel sorry for the teams we beat,' Sione continued. 'They've been waiting for this for ages, just like we have.'

They looked up as Izzy walked into the room. 'Ah, I thought I'd find you guys in here,' he chuckled, shaking his head. 'Early lights out tonight, everyone. Let's go.'

For once, no one protested. The bats and balls were abandoned and everyone slowly filed out into the hall.

'We'll make it to the semis, won't we?' Daniel said as he passed Izzy.

'It's always best to think positive,' Izzy replied with a wink.

Daniel nodded. 'We will. You'll see,' he said confidently.

DANIEL

While everyone dressed and prepared for their final game in the first round of the competition, Izzy moved what he could to clear a space in the change room for the boys to jog on the spot.

'After two games yesterday, everyone needs to be loose and ready,' he said. 'There will be distractions on the field, so I'd like you to warm up here first.'

The team jogged on the spot and performed dynamic stretches.

'When will we get to play in the main stadium?' Adam asked as he jumped on and off a bench at one end of the room. 'I bet the change rooms are even bigger there.'

'Just worry about this game,' Daniel said, puffing. 'If we win we'll get to play in the semis — our ticket to the big stadium.'

'Everything all right in here?' Tom Parker asked, popping his head into the room.

Izzy nodded and smiled. 'Yep, we're just about ready.'

'Okay, good luck, everyone!' Tom called, giving them a thumbs up before disappearing into the hallway again.

Izzy clapped to get everyone's attention. 'Grab your gear, guys. It's showtime,' he yelled. 'Remember the basics and play hard. Don't think about finals yet, just focus on the hurdle in front of you.'

At Izzy's direction, Daniel put on his headgear. This was almost a ceremony for him now – it was the last thing he did before going onto the field. When he'd first started wearing the headgear, it had seemed cumbersome, but now he didn't feel right without it. He tightened the straps under his chin and walked to the door. He propped it open and looked down the short hallway that led to the field.

The first thing Daniel noticed was the noise – the constant hum of the crowd was louder than the day before. The first thing

Jake noticed wasn't the sound, but the smell of the barbecue that was cooking at the back of the stands.

'Don't even think about it,' Sione said, reading his mind.

Jake lowered his head, and Daniel and Sione laughed.

'If you're hungry, go for carbs, not grease,' Daniel said. 'First, we have a game to win.'

As they walked onto the field one after another, the crowd cheered.

Sione's stomach dropped when he saw who they'd be playing against. It was the blue team. *They* were South Shore. All of them had their arms folded as they watched Valley do a lap of the pitch.

Oh great, Daniel thought.

'This is going to be terrible,' Sione muttered.

Daniel fought the urge to agree. 'Come on, guys,' he said. 'We're one win away from being undefeated and probably getting the top seed going into the finals. Worry about our game, not their faces.'

That seemed to do the trick. There was no more discussion, and when they rounded the last corner to take part in the anthem and coin toss, no one even looked at the South Shore players.

Daniel won the coin toss and, remembering his father's advice, he called the team around him before they set themselves for the kick-off. 'Uh . . . okay, guys, play well!' he said. 'We can do this!'

Jake laughed. 'You gathered us around for that? We know *that*!'

Daniel blushed. 'Look, just stay focused and have fun.'

Everyone in the team nodded in agreement. Two weeks ago many of them would have put Daniel in his place and called him bossy or a show-off. Today, they clapped and ran to their positions.

'Let's do this!' Jake shouted.

'Do what?' Mick yelled from the other side of the halfway line. 'Lose?'

Daniel didn't know everything about being a good captain, but he knew the way Mick was doing it was wrong. He kicked the ball towards South Shore and the game was on.

Mick caught the ball easily and passed it to another player, who ran at Daniel. Daniel tackled him but couldn't bring him down. He pushed Daniel backwards, carrying the ball with him. Daniel managed to stay on his feet and was soon joined in the struggle by Adam and Tezza. But the South Shore boy had helpers too. Soon, a gigantic rucking contest began, the ball creeping towards South Shore's tryline, still being carried by the South Shore player.

He was eventually taken down, but South Shore regathered and passed the ball out to the wing. Daniel stood up and found himself face to face with Mick.

'*That's* how you do it,' Mick said, 'and we don't need someone famous to tell us that.'

Daniel ignored him and ran after the play, trying to stay focused on the game. The South Shore winger was tackled but his team retained possession for a very long passage of offence. They settled for a field-goal attempt that was kicked truly, putting South Shore in front three points to nil.

Daniel groaned.

'Maybe you need a new coach,' Mick snarled as he ran past.

Daniel frowned and glanced over at the bench. Izzy looked back at him, shaking his head. Daniel knew Izzy wanted him to rise above Mick's rudeness.

Sione jogged up to Daniel. 'Ignore him,' he whispered. 'He's only saying that stuff to put you off.'

'I don't get it,' Daniel said. 'If you're good enough to beat us, fine, but the game we're playing is called rugby, not teasing.'

'So let's beat them at rugby,' said Sione.

Daniel looked up at the stands. His dad was there, still not in green, still sitting on his own and looking straight at his son. Daniel wondered what he was thinking. Was he blaming Daniel for Valley falling behind on the scoreboard?

On Valley's first extended period with the ball it became pretty clear that South Shore didn't want to just tackle them, they wanted to hurt them. Their tackles were harder than he had ever felt before. Soon Daniel was covered in dirt and grass stains.

'Enjoying it?' Mick asked at one point.

Daniel just smiled in response. But the comments kept coming. They were sometimes about Izzy, sometimes about Daniel and his teammates. Sometimes they were whispered, sometimes yelled.

'Our coach has way more experience than yours,' Mick taunted. 'He's no flash in the pan – he used to be a real star.'

He's just jealous, Daniel told himself over and over again. But by doing so he lost his focus. Once Valley had finally made good field position, Daniel received the ball and dropped it forward. It was a knock-on.

Mick laughed and pointed at Daniel. 'Some captain!'

Daniel clenched his fists. 'Are you here to play the game or to just put us off ours?'

he yelled. But this just made Mick laugh harder.

The scrum formed and South Shore won it. Daniel got himself into position. He knew Mick was about to receive the ball from their scrum-half. Daniel wanted to tackle him – and hard.

He snapped off his position and flew towards the opposing captain. In the micro-seconds before his tackle landed, Daniel's mind scanned its stores of knowledge for every-thing he had ever learnt about tackling – approach side-on, go for the body first, watch your posture. When his body clashed with Mick's, there was little chance of injury and every chance of success.

But Mick was too big and too strong. It felt like tackling a wall – a moving wall that grunted and then turned and laughed as it powered towards the tryline.

On the ground, with dirt on his face and feeling as if he'd just been run over by a steam roller, Daniel looked up. He saw TJ, Valley's last line of defence, bounce off Mick like a balloon. Daniel closed his eyes and hung his head. He wished it was all over. He wished he could hide. He wished he'd never even come on the tour.

SIONE

'We did it! We did it!' Jake shouted once they made it to the change rooms after the game. 'We're in the finals!'

That should have been the cue for everyone to start shouting and stomping. An announcement like that was supposed to get the room bubbling over with energy, but the only cheering Sione could hear was coming from the South Shore change room next door.

South Shore had made Sione feel like a kid who didn't even know how to play rugby. After losing by fourteen points, he certainly didn't feel like he belonged on a rep team. Sione could think of hundreds of ways he could have played better. He slumped in the corner of the room, trying his best not to think about the fact his family had watched the game.

'You should be happy,' Jake said, thumping him on the back. 'Come on, everyone – we're in the finals!'

But, like the others, Sione wasn't ready to shout and stamp. He had to think this through.

Izzy and Jeremy walked into the room carrying the team's gear. The silence hung heavy in the air.

'I know it's hard, guys,' Izzy said, dropping a bag of balls on the floor. 'It feels terrible to lose. But I am proud of you. You all did your best and you deserve your spot in the semis.'

'Wait, so what Jake is saying is true?' Daniel asked.

Izzy nodded. 'We came second in our group of four. The top two teams from each group make the semis.'

'Just don't tell me we have to play *them* again,' said Adam.

Izzy shook his head. 'We play a team from the other group.'

'But if we make the Grand Final we'll have to play South Shore again, won't we?' Daniel said.

'Yes,' Izzy replied. 'You'll have to play them if they win their semi-final.'

'See? We *are* in the finals!' Jake said excitedly.

The boys gathered around their coach, all of them buzzing about how they had made it into the final four.

Izzy laughed. 'Now I know what it's like living in a beehive!' he said. Everyone settled a little and gave him some space. 'I know today was tough – and that's okay. We must learn from it, though, and move on and continue to play our best rugby this afternoon. I know we can do it.'

'By the way,' Jeremy piped up, 'the final first-round match was just completed over on the main ground. Would you like to know who our opponents will be in the semis?'

'Of course!' Daniel said, and the rest of the boys nodded.

'As you know, the top two teams from each group play the second-placed teams from the other group to mix it up a bit,' Jeremy continued.

'Yeah, so who are we playing?' Adam asked. The anticipation was making him nervous.

Jeremy laughed. 'We'll be playing River Region this afternoon, and the other game will be Western Plains versus South Shore.'

'South Shore's match is on before ours, so I thought we could go and watch it to see what playing in the main stadium is like,' Izzy suggested.

'But they are horrible, mean players,' said Harrison. 'They don't deserve a finals spot.'

TJ shook his head. 'I can't believe we might have to play them again,' he said wearily.

'Now wait a second,' said Izzy. 'We should be immensely proud about making the finals. We deserve our spot and South Shore earnt theirs as well. They're a hard team, but now we know what to expect. We can do it.'

'Don't let your fears defeat you,' Jeremy added, loading some witch's hats into a large, netted bag.

Sione sat down, deflated once again. But Daniel seemed to stand up even taller.

'That's right,' he said, raising his voice for everyone to hear. 'Come on, Valley, don't be afraid. We can do this! First things first — we have a semi-final to play this evening. I'm going to run my guts out because I want our names written on that trophy!'

Sione smiled. He was glad that Daniel had been chosen to be their captain.

'Daniel's right,' said Izzy. 'Let's celebrate our performance after the competition is over. We have to stay focused for the next game — the game you've earnt your place in. It isn't for a few hours, so let's do some stretches, stay warm and have a rest while we watch the other match.'

Sione looked around the main stadium in awe as he walked out onto the tiered seating. They were much higher up than he had expected. The grandstand went right around the ground; it felt more like a bowl than a football field. Every noise from the crowd echoed around them. This was legit.

'I can't wait to play down there,' Daniel said as they sat down to watch the game.

'But would you want to play down there *with them*?' Sione asked. He pointed at South Shore, who were handing out one hard-hitting tackle after another. They were meeting the Western Plains offence so hard that Sione could hear and feel every tackle from way up in the stands.

'Of course,' Daniel answered. 'We're going to beat them next time.'

The game against River Region began before Sione was ready for it. This competition didn't seem to give them any time to think. All of a sudden, there he was in his green jersey, running, passing and tackling a team from a part of the state Sione had never even heard of before.

The sun dropped lower in the sky as the game wore on. This was a semi-final and everyone seemed to have increased their desire to win accordingly. Despite it being both team's fourth match in two days, no one gave up from exhaustion. They just pushed on.

At half-time, Izzy pulled Sione aside. 'I'm putting you on as hooker,' he said.

'No!' Sione gasped before he could control himself. 'I'm sorry, Izzy,' he said after he'd composed himself. 'I just want to play where I'm best. This is the semis.'

'And we need you in the forwards,' Izzy said firmly. 'Everyone is sore – especially Adam. His foot still isn't a hundred per cent, though he'd like you to think it is. You'll be helping out the team. Adam needs a rest.'

Sione nodded. He understood, but that didn't mean he had to like it.

'Remember on the Gold Coast when you fought the idea so hard? You found your way in the end, didn't you?'

Sione looked up at his coach. *How does Izzy always find a way to turn a bad situation good?* 'Okay,' he sighed. 'If the team needs me to.'

Izzy smiled. 'That's the spirit! Thanks, Sione. You'll be great.' Izzy winked at him then ran over to gather the rest of the team together.

Sione took a deep breath, trying to get into the right head space for his new position. He hadn't even thought about the score. He was bruised and battered and the world seemed blurry. He knew they had been playing well, but how well?

'What's the score?' he whispered to Daniel.

'Are you kidding me?' Daniel laughed. 'You don't know?'

Sione shook his head. 'We've been running upfield away from the scoreboard and I was kind of too afraid to look.'

'We're in front thirty-one to seven. Wake up!'

Sione gasped. He had no idea they were playing that well! He puffed out his chest and ran into position with a burst of new-found energy.

Sione seamlessly transitioned into his role as hooker, drawing on what he had learnt the week before, and it helped that Valley were already so far in front. Valley played smooth and tough in every play, and River Region continued to falter. As the sky darkened and the stadium lights came on, the scoreboard showed they had almost doubled their half-time score. Sione couldn't believe it.

What was even harder to believe were the events after a scrum near the Valley tryline. Sione put his head down when the scrum engaged, and after the River Region scrum-half fed the ball into it, he helped to push the scrum forward so strongly that he soon saw the white paint of the tryline beneath his feet. The ball bounced around in the scrum like popcorn in a pan. Sione managed to scoop it up with his foot and push it backwards.

'It's out!' Harrison shouted, and the scrum disintegrated.

Valley had won the ball against the feed!

Jake managed to gain possession of it and steamed towards the line but was held up above it by a number of defenders. Sione charged into the pack, pushing Jake and the others over the line. Jake reached out and planted the point of the ball in the grass.

The team went beserk.

Sione looked up into the stands and was greeted with the sight of green streamers unfurling through the air and banners waving frantically. He could see his dad pumping his fist. Daniel wrapped his arms around Sione and gave Jake a high five. Sione knew then that nothing would ever compare to this.

DANIEL

'I'm wrecked!' Daniel said, collapsing onto a sofa. He stretched his entire body out along the cushions.

'Hey!' Adam yelled. 'Make room for us, you chair hog.'

Daniel reluctantly pulled up his legs, allowing Sione and Adam to sit down.

Jake and the others were sitting on chairs or spread out across the floor. The entire team had brought blankets and sleeping bags from their rooms and were now either lying down or nodding their heads as they sat, fighting the urge to sleep. All twenty players were sore, bruised and drained of energy but ecstatic, too.

'You know what's terrible?' said Adam. 'Tomorrow is the State Championships final, and the next day we have to go to –'

'Ugh! Don't say it!' Daniel groaned.

'– school.'

Jake covered his ears. 'Shhh! You're ruining my night!'

Jeremy, Tom, Mary and Izzy had set up their own little camp sites around the room.

Everyone sat facing a giant screen on the back wall. Usually used for slide show presentations during seminars or conventions, tonight it was Valley's personal movie screen.

Izzy stood up and made his way to the front of the room. 'As you all know, this will be our last night together,' he said sombrely.

Daniel swallowed.

'The last two weeks have been special – transformative,' Izzy continued. 'I will never forget this trip, and it's not because of all the fun things we did, places we saw or games we played. It's because of you. You're a great bunch of boys and I wish you all luck in your rugby careers.'

For the first time in ages, Daniel could feel his eyes welling up. He wiped his face.

Tom and Mary stood up next. 'We have kids of our own,' said Tom, 'but they are grown up now. This trip has been a pleasure for us. It's been lots of hard work, but spending time with you boys has also been lots of fun.'

'Just remember to pack your bags well in the morning,' added Mary. 'There'll be no lost property!'

Daniel and the others laughed.

'It's been great managing this tour,' said Jeremy. 'Your behaviour has been impeccable. I've seen you grow as a team, as rugby players and as young men. Win, lose or draw tomorrow, we are proud of you. That being said, I do have a feeling you will win.' He gave them a wink and sat down.

Should I, as captain, get up and make a speech? Daniel wondered. *Does Izzy want me to, or will the other boys think I'm a massive try-hard?*

Izzy looked over at Daniel and flicked his head towards the front of the room. That was all the invitation Daniel needed. He stood up and walked to the front.

'Thank you to all the adults for a great tour,' he said, his voice trembling. 'It's been lots of fun and I won't forget anyone here, either. I think I might have made some new best friends, which is pretty cool.'

Daniel took a deep breath. There was more he wanted to say. He hoped the words came out of his mouth right.

'I started this tour thinking that I should be captain. I thought I was the best player here and I hadn't even seen any of you guys play before.' His eyes dropped down to his feet. 'I'm sorry.'

Daniel looked up to see Izzy smiling at him and he found the strength to keep going.

'I know that if I had been made captain on day one I would have stuffed it up. All of you would've hated me. I was . . . difficult and headstrong. But over the last couple of weeks I feel I have grown a lot – both on and off the field – and it's because of you guys. I am so proud that tomorrow, when we run out for the Grand Final, I will be your captain. Thanks for everything.'

Everyone clapped and, as Daniel made his way back to his seat, the boys patted him on the back. A few other kids took his lead and said a few words. A warmth washed over Daniel. He knew this night would be something he would never forget. This feeling became even clearer when Sione, the last person Daniel would have ever expected to stand in front of the group, got up.

'Um . . .' Sione began. 'I've never done a speech before, even at school. I can't do them, but . . . I can tonight, I think. I was shy before the tour – and scared. I still am, but I know everyone here is my friend. I didn't know that before. I think on tour I have learnt that usually everyone is nicer than you expect. My rugby's better, too.'

Everyone clapped harder and louder than for any of the other speakers. Izzy stood up and gave Sione a high five. Soon the lights were turned off and the movie began. Within ten minutes, most of the boys were sound asleep. Daniel looked around at his teammates, visible in the flickering glow of the projector screen, and smiled.

Then, unexpectedly, his phone vibrated. Daniel wriggled it out of his pocket and saw that he had an email from his mum. He took a deep breath and opened it.

His mum began the email by saying how proud she was of Daniel and apologising for not replying sooner. She explained that a flight from Perth at short notice was tricky and that she wouldn't be able to make it to the tournament. Though it was sad news, Daniel smiled as he read it, especially when he got to the end:

Good luck, Daniel. I'm sure you will do well. Write back and tell me how it goes.

Love, Mum.

Daniel read the email over and over again. *She cares*, he thought, *and she does love me.* He felt calm, like he didn't have a worry in the world, and hoped he might see her again soon.

 SIONE

Sione had heard people say they had butterflies in their stomach, but he'd never
understood what the saying meant until
today. Being nervous usually made him
feel sick. But now, as he was about to
run out onto the field for the Grand Final,
he finally got it. The mix of nervousness

and anticipation felt like a thousand little butterfly wings flickering inside him.

The feeling had begun earlier in the morning at a thank-you morning tea for the players' families organised by Izzy, Jeremy and the Parkers. A small room had been reserved for all the players and parents to mingle before the big game. As soon as Sione saw his family, the butterflies began to stir.

They had stood around chatting for what seemed like forever. There were hundreds of questions about the trip as Mele raced around the room and Sione ate more than his fair share of egg sandwiches. He'd laughed when Aunty tried to discuss their plans for gathering Sione's belongings and the journey home.

'Please, Aunty,' he'd said, 'I can't talk about that now. I just need to focus on the game.' He knew she was just trying to be organised, but with the biggest game of his life about to start, Sione didn't want to worry about what time their train was leaving.

Izzy had wandered over and shook hands with Sione's dad. They also exchanged a few words in their native Tongan. Sione didn't quite catch it, but his dad's face lit up as they spoke. They ended up laughing and bumping fists, which pleased Sione. He'd never seen his dad relax and talk to other people like that. He wasn't even sure his dad had any friends. *Maybe Dad and Izzy will become best mates!* Sione thought excitedly.

Sione had held back asking about his mum for the entire morning tea, but when it came time to go, he couldn't keep it to himself any longer. 'Aunty?' he said softly. 'Is Mum going to come and watch the game?'

'Oh, Sione,' Aunty said, holding out her arms to hug him, 'I don't even know how to reach her. The number I have just rings out. I'm so sorry.'

Sione nodded and hugged her back, letting his aunty's green shirt soak up his tears. 'It's okay,' he said eventually, pulling away. 'Thanks for trying. I'm glad you're here anyway.'

'I'm glad to be here,' Aunty said gently. She took a tissue from her pocket and dabbed at his cheeks.

Now, in the change rooms, Sione couldn't sit still. He paced back and forth along the length of the room. He even clapped and jumped as he walked. There was so much energy inside him he felt like he'd burst if he sat down.

Yet, the rest of his team was sitting down. It was as if everyone's personalities had flipped. Sione was usually the one sitting quietly in the corner amid the chaos before a game. Today, he was the chaos.

Izzy came up beside Sione. 'It's okay to feel nervous,' he said, 'or however you feel. Just let your feelings happen.'

Sione nodded.

'Remember when you found me doing my morning training on the first day of the tour?'

Sione nodded again.

'From that moment I knew you were destined for great things on the field. You showed your enthusiasm and dedication that morning and every morning you trained with me on tour. Those are two things you need to have to do well.'

'Thanks,' Sione said, suddenly shy.

'And you have shown so many great skills on the field. You've been hard at it in pretty much every game. Just yesterday, the way you stepped into the forward line and helped us score that try – well, you're great.'

This is amazing but why is Izzy saying all this now? Sione wondered.

'So, after today, I want you to remember that. You *are* great. Wherever you go and whatever you do, be proud of yourself and try your best.'

Sione wished he could ask Izzy to write those words down so he would never forget them. 'Yes, Izzy.'

'Good stuff, mate.'

Sione sat down, the weight of Izzy's words too great to hold up.

Izzy clapped his hands to get everyone's attention. The twenty Valley boys dressed in green stared up at him, their eyes wide and ready for any encouraging words their coach had to say.

'There's not much that I can add to what you already know,' Izzy began. 'You know to try your best, to play hard, to remember our training. You know how to play – you just need to do it.

'So, all I want to tell you is: enjoy yourselves. Soak it all in, never forget it. Be happy you are here no matter the result. And, of course, don't come off the oval with regrets. I want you to be able to smile when you look back on this experience, even if we lose.'

Sione knew he wouldn't be leaving with regrets. He was going to play his best – the best he'd ever played. He was going to run, pass and tackle non-stop. Sione also knew he was going to cherish the memory of the tour, if only because he had done it all with Izzy. He had learnt so much from his mentor and coach.

The boys ran out of the change room and up to the ground for the final time as a team. They burst through the banner of green crepe-paper streamers. Sione blinked as the sun shone in his eyes. He held up his arm to shade his face and saw the blue banner on the opposite side of the ground. He looked up at the stands as they ran their lap.

The bowl-like stadium was completely full. Not only was everyone's family there in force, but the six teams not playing in the final were there, too. And the crowd was loud – *really* loud. It gave Sione goosebumps.

Sione searched for his family and found them in a patch of green shirts, flags and streamers, sitting almost perpendicular to the halfway line. Sione waved up at them and he saw Mele point and wave back.

Daniel won the coin toss and signalled that he wanted to kick off. Then the Valley captain called everyone in for a team huddle. But this time he didn't try to excite them with a pep talk. In fact, he said nothing about the game at all.

'I just wanted to say this in case I don't get the chance later,' he shouted to the circle of

Valley players. 'Tomorrow we're still friends. Tomorrow we are still Valley. This might be our last match but it isn't the end of *us*.'

Sione looked straight at Daniel, agreeing wholeheartedly with each word.

'But right now,' Daniel added, 'we have a job to do.'

'Let's go, Valley!' Jake shouted, and the team stretched out along the ground to face South Shore.

DANIEL

Daniel stood in the centre of the field, holding the ball. He looked out across the field at Mick, who stared back, his shoulders rising and falling with each breath. Daniel could imagine him snarling like an angry dog.

'Ready to lose again?' Mick shouted. 'This is going to be so easy!'

Daniel looked away. He wasn't going to let the South Shore boys put him off his game this time. He cleared the memory of their previous match from his mind. All that mattered was now, and he wanted to ensure that good rugby won the game, not taunts and heckling.

'Don't let them intimidate you, boys,' Daniel called to his left, down the Valley line. He turned to his right. 'We can win!'

Daniel kicked the ball. It was a short one, designed to put South Shore under pressure from the start. Mick gathered the ball himself and chuffed towards the Valley line, which was already upon him.

Jake and Adam smacked into him hard. The crowd audibly cringed in response.

The Valley supporters cheered once they realised Mick had knocked-on, coughing out the ball from the pound of the tackle.

It took Jake and Adam a while to get up from the tangle of limbs on the ground, but when they finally did, Mick stayed down, clutching his arm and rolling from side to side.

'They injured me,' he wailed, 'on purpose!'

'Pe-nal-ty! Pe-nal-ty!' the South Shore boys chanted.

Jake and Adam ran over to plead their case to the ref. Daniel's mind was swimming. *What's happening?* he thought. *Mick clearly knocked-on! He's just trying to distract us.*

The referee held up his hand and told Mick to get off the ground if he was injured. Once it was clear no penalty was coming, Mick rose to his feet and winked at Daniel. Designed to anger him, the wink only did the opposite – it made Daniel want to play even harder.

But a few minutes later it was the blue team that scored. A hard-fought try and conversion had them up seven to nil. Daniel was concerned. He was able to ignore the menacing tactics of South Shore, but could his teammates?

After getting the ball back from another kick-off by Daniel, South Shore were set upon by Valley. Tackle, scrum, line-out, kick – the Crocs did everything to perfection and by the book.

We are a true team now, Daniel thought proudly. *Nothing can put us off our game.*

A few minutes before half-time, the South Shore frustrations rose to an all-time high when one of their centres tackled Steven around the neck. As he walked off the field, Daniel saw the rest of the South Shore team huddle around the tackler to congratulate him. This made Daniel's blood boil, but he calmed himself and placed the ball on his kicking tee. He was going to get back at them in the best way.

He kicked the penalty goal, taking Valley to three to seven in the first half.

The sound of the crowd filtered into the change room. It was difficult to focus on

Izzy with all the noise they were making, but Daniel wasn't going to let anything stand in the way of his team's success. He leant in closer to hear what his coach had to say.

'I've got two things for you, boys,' Izzy said. 'First, I want us to kick the ball high whenever we have the opportunity. They don't look confident under the high ball. Maybe they'll drop one or two, we'll see.'

Daniel and the rest of the team nodded.

'Also, I want to stress the importance of keeping our defensive line tight. No gaps, no holes. You should be running as hard as the attackers – or even harder! Keep together, move sideways to follow the ball. I know you're tired, but you can sleep in the car on the way home.' One or two boys laughed at that. 'You're doing great. Remember that you have half a game left. Let's keep it up!'

The team clapped and filed out of the room, still digesting Izzy's advice.

The ball went deep early in the second half, and the backs got set for an offensive drive led by Daniel. They moved the ball quickly, running hard and passing strong. South Shore clearly didn't like it when they weren't in possession. Daniel could tell by the increase of verbal attacks that were coming their way.

'Give us the ball,' Mick shouted once, 'so we don't have to hurt you in a tackle!'

Valley kept possession for a long time, but South Shore's tackling was ferocious and it was hard to make any progress upfield.

Eventually, Daniel decided it was time for a change. He received the ball and kicked it high towards their fullback.

Valley stormed after the ball, each player wanting to put Izzy's plan into action. They pressured the South Shore fullback by their very presence and he fumbled the ball. Tezza dove on it, regaining possession for Valley.

'Come on!' Mick shouted at his players. 'They aren't good enough to beat us!'

The game continued. Daniel grew tired and emotionally distant. It had been a tough slog – this game and the entire tour – and as he was nearing the end, his energy was waning. Yet, he couldn't stop. He couldn't bear to let his team down. He played in silence, not hearing a thing besides his own breath. The voices of others were muffled, the ball almost non-existent in his hands.

Tackle after tackle, pass after pass, Daniel felt like a robot. He knew what he had to do and his body did it without prompting. Nothing got through to his senses, especially not South Shore's teasing. It was as if the game were being played in slow motion and Daniel had all the time in the world to pass a ball or gather it from the ground.

He passed the ball to Sione but seemed to catch it again five minutes later. He turned and looked upfield, his breathing now as loud as thunder. He watched Sione sidestep a defender and then, with a zip, run to the tryline and dive over the line.

With a whoosh like water being sucked down a plughole, the sounds of the game returned, swirling all around Daniel as he leapt into the air, screaming. The Valley supporters jumped to their feet, cheering, as Sione stood up clutching the ball.

Daniel ran over and lifted him high like a line-out forward, Sione pumping his fists in the air. Soon they were surrounded by the rest of their teammates. Daniel looked up at the crowd. His dad was jumping up and down with the other parents, cheering more than Daniel had ever seen him cheer, which made the try even sweeter.

The referee reminded Daniel of his conversion attempt. Daniel smiled with glee as he ran to set up the kick, leaving his team

to continue celebrating their try. He went through the motions and slotted the kick easily, putting Valley in front by ten points to seven. But in the end those extra two points didn't matter. Seconds after restarting play, the siren blew. Daniel reached for the sky, not wanting the siren to stop.

Arms swung around him as he was hugged on all sides by his teammates. A wave of green-shirted supporters ran onto the field, surrounding the team and cheering 'Go, Crocs! Go, Crocs!' Daniel laughed, no longer knowing which way was up.

A hand reached through and grabbed Daniel, pulling him close. His dad embraced him tight for the first time in years and Daniel let him.

'You played so well!' his dad yelled above the noise. 'I am so, so proud of you. So proud!'

Daniel looked up at his father and smiled, before they were jostled apart by the crowd. 'Where's Izzy?' he asked. His dad pointed over Daniel's shoulder. Daniel turned around to see his coach running to him. 'We did it, Izzy! We did it!' he yelled.

'Yes, we did,' Izzy said, grinning from ear to ear. He gave Daniel a high five and they held up each other's hands in triumph.

Daniel scanned the crowded field for Sione. He finally spotted him and jogged over. 'You played amazing,' Daniel said proudly.

'Are you kidding?' Sione replied, incredulous. '*You* were the greatest!'

'We did it! Can you believe it?' Daniel laughed.

Sione nodded. 'This is exactly how I want to remember today. It's perfect.'

Sione knelt down and and pulled out a clump of soggy paper from one of his socks. 'Look, Mele,' he called, 'I kept your drawing!'

Daniel pulled a face. 'Oh, man, that's gross!'

Mele ran up to her big brother and hugged him around the waist. 'Don't worry,' she said, looking over at Daniel. 'I can draw one for you for the next game.'

Daniel grinned. 'Why not tomorrow after school?'

Mele giggled and skipped back to her aunty and father.

Sione looked at Daniel. 'You mean it? You're gonna come over?'

'Of course,' Daniel said, 'and I'm bringing my new trophy with me!'

SIONE TAITO

POSITION: Wing

SCHOOL: Valley North

TEAM: The Tigers

LOVES TO: Watch Izzy Folau play on TV

Picked to play for the Valley team on the wing, Sione has many attributes that good wingers need. He is fast, fit and able to find a gap within any line of defence. At first, Sione wasn't sure if playing on a rep team was the right fit for him, but since finding his feet with Valley, he has become more comfortable with his selection.

Soft-spoken Sione does all his 'talking' on the rugby field, where he strives to play with the enthusiasm and happiness of his hero, Izzy Folau. Sione plays for the Tigers in his local competition. There, he has excelled and become what many rugby fans might call a 'try-scoring machine', though those are words he would never use to describe himself.

DANIEL MASTERS

POSITION: Fly-half

SCHOOL: Barton Grammar

TEAM: Barton Grammar

LOVES TO: Kick a match-winning goal

Daniel plays for Valley at the vital position of fly-half. As he directs the back line on the field, he also tries hard to lead by example off the field. Daniel's ultimate dream is to captain Australia at the Rugby World Cup. Sometimes his dedication and desire to win get in the way of having a good time, but with Valley, he is learning to do both.

Daniel is also a terrific goal kicker who is never happier than after kicking one hundred per cent of his attempts in a match. His success comes from the extra hard work he puts in after training and on his days off. If there ever was a boy who loved his rugby, it's Daniel. Possibly the most passionate rugby player in the world after Izzy Folau, Daniel never stops giving his all.

VALLEY TEAM

Name: Daniel Masters

Position: Fly-half

Plays for: Barton Grammar

Known for: His accurate goal kicking

Greatest moment: Leading his team to an undefeated season

Name: Sione 'the Eel' Taito

Position: Wing

Plays for: The Tigers

Known for: Weaving through defenders

Greatest moment: Being selected for the Valley rep team

Name: Theo 'TJ' Jones

Position: Fullback

Plays for: Grantham Boys

Known for: Catching high balls under pressure

Greatest moment: Scoring three tries in a grand final

Name: Steven Hendricks

Position: Wing

Plays for: The Bears

Known for: His courage under pressure

Greatest moment: Scoring a try in his first game

Name: Eric Le

Position: Centre

Plays for: Saxby Prep

Known for: Being selected for Valley in his first year playing rugby

Greatest moment: Scoring a hundred-metre try

Name: Joseph Rosenberg

Position: Centre

Plays for: Saxby Prep

Known for: His ability to set up tries

Greatest moment: Putting five other teammates on the scoreboard in one game

Name: Harrison Gordon

Position: Scrum-half

Plays for: Bunyan Bunyips

Known for: His leadership at the scrum

Greatest moment: Winning his team's Best Player trophy two years in a row

Name: Derek 'the Ringmaster' Ngo

Position: Wing

Plays for: Clifton Grammar

Known for: Running rings around the opposition

Greatest moment: Being promoted from the D Team to the A Team at school within two weeks

Name: Ty Fennelly

Position: Fullback

Plays for: St Francis's

Known for: His long kick returns

Greatest moment: Scoring twenty-five points in one match

Name: Jake Hunter

Position: Prop

Plays for: Queens

Known for: His strong tackling

Greatest moment: Playing every minute of every game last season

Name: Benny Simons

Position: Prop

Plays for: Queens

Known for: Pushing opposition teams back in the scrum

Greatest moment: Being selected for two different rep teams in two different states

Name: Adam El-Attar

Position: Hooker

Plays for: St Christopher's

Known for: His jumping in the line-out

Greatest moment: Making thirty tackles in one game

Name: Tim Broadbent

Position: Second row

Plays for: The Saints

Known for: His goal kicking

Greatest moment: His tackle in extra time that saved his team's season

Name: Patrick Mulholland

Position: Second row

Plays for: The Saints

Known for: Taking on any opponent, no matter how big

Greatest moment: Chasing down an opponent from twenty metres behind, then tackling him into touch

Name: Terry 'Tezza' Williams

Position: Flanker

Plays for: The Bears

Known for: His speed down the blind side

Greatest moment: Scoring a try in every game last season

Name: Zach Smith

Position: Flanker

Plays for: St Francis's

Known for: His ability to play as a forward or back

Greatest moment: Being his team's captain and also its youngest player

Name: Nathan Davidson

Position: Number-eight

Plays for: Clifton Grammar

Known for: His seemingly unlimited energy

Greatest moment: Regularly landing twenty-metre-long passes to teammates

Name: Kane Williams

Position: Utility-forward

Plays for: The Saints

Known for: His accurate kicking for touch

Greatest moment: Playing in every forward position last season

Name: Sean de Groot

Position: Utility-forward

Plays for: Clifton Grammar

Known for: His 'never give up' attitude

Greatest moment: Winning a grand final with an extra-time try

Name: Kian Hardy

Position: Utility-forward

Plays for: Clifton Grammar

Known for: Always walking off the field covered in mud

Greatest moment: He has played for three Premiership-winning teams

ISRAEL FOLAU

NICKNAME: Izzy

BORN: 3 April 1989 in Minto, NSW

HEIGHT: 195 cm

WEIGHT: 103 kg

POSITION: Fullback

TEAM: NSW Waratahs, Australian Wallabies

IZZY'S CAREER

2007/08: NRL Melbourne Storm

2007–2009: Australian Kangaroos

2008–2010: Queensland Maroons

2009/10: NRL Brisbane Broncos

2010: NRL All Stars

2011/2012: AFL Greater Western Sydney Giants

2013–present: NSW Waratahs

2013–present: Australian Wallabies

IZZY'S TRAINING TIPS: TACKLING

Tackling is one of the most obvious features of a rugby match. Not only does tackling stop the opposition in their tracks, it often causes them to turn over the ball. Each player will perform many tackles in a game, so it is something that everyone needs to practise regularly. Without a good tackling technique, ball-carriers will break through your defensive line and there is a greater possibility of injury. With proper training, every player can make effective tackles, whatever their size and strength.

There are four things to remember in order to tackle properly.

1) Be ready.

- Keep your eyes open at all times. Know who you are tackling and where on their body you will be making contact. Be alert.

- Keep your head up. Don't duck or bend your neck as the runner approaches.

- Keep your back straight. If your spine is aligned, you will reduce the risk of hurting yourself.

2) Make contact with your shoulder.

- Approach the tackle with the leg and shoulder on the side of your body nearest to your opponent.

- Let your shoulder land on your opponent first, then wrap your arms around them. If you only use your arms, your tackle will have no stability or strength.

3) Use your knees.

- Bend your knees in preparation for the tackle.

- Your strength should come through your knees, not your upper body. Be stable and be strong.

4) Keep your toes close.

- The closer your big toe is to the tackle, the better it will be, because the closer you are the more likely your shoulder will engage. Don't be afraid to be close to the ball-carrier.

If you are unsure about your technique, practise tackling some padding before trying it out in a real game. Find your confidence. A weak tackle is a waste of time, so make sure you commit to it one hundred per cent. Be strong and do your best!

Here are tips for when you have mastered the basics.

- Step to one side as the ball-carrier approaches you. Tackling them in motion is more effective than tackling them from a standing position.

- Make the tackle as early as possible.

- Worry about the ball *after* you have landed your tackle, not before. Focus on stopping the player first.

Remember: Tackling should only be practised under the supervision of your coach or other responsible adults.

COLLECT THE SERIES

OUT NOW